Loch Ness Monster

The Legendary Stories of the Loch Ness Monster from an Unbiased View

Table of Contents

Introduction

This short, concise book contains information regarding the origins of the famous Nessie, how the legend came to be, and a few explanations and theories that attempt to shed some light on whether this magnificent creature is real or a product of man's collective wishful thinking. Our aim here is to be objective and not pass any bias to try and persuade readers into believing or not believing.

Since the dawn of time, humans have been weary of the unknown things that lurked beneath the dark, murky waters of the world. The people that lived near the majestic Loch Ness were no different, and for generations their kin told stories of a beast that ruled the great lake, swimming just under the surface of the water, watching for any who might dare enter its domain.

It is no surprise that the unknowable mysteries of the deep still intrigue us today. The Loch Ness Monster has become an icon of the possibility of something unknown — something undiscovered. Are the legends true? Do the myriad of sightings, blurry photographs, and video evidence really prove that Nessie is out there? You will have to judge for yourself.

Thanks again for grabbing this book, we hope you enjoy it!

Chapter 1:

The Legend of Nessie

In the Scottish highlands, there is a particularly large freshwater lake that is said to be the home of one of modern history's most famous and most hotly debated cryptids. The lake is called Loch Ness—its name originating from its old Scottish Gaelic name *Loch Nis*, meaning "Lake Ness."

Loch Ness is a huge body of water extending roughly twenty-three miles along the heart of Scotland, flowing out to the sea through the city of Inverness further northeast. It has a width of about three kilometers and has an average depth of about a hundred and thirty meters, although some parts can reach depths that are almost twice its average, which is somewhere around two hundred and thirty meters.

Beneath these depths is said to live a cryptid that has captured the imagination of the residents around the lake and, indeed, the entire world. Even with the lack of evidence regarding the creature's existence, locals have taken to affectionately call her *Nessie*. To the rest of the world, the beast is known as the Loch Ness Monster.

Although accounts somewhat vary, Nessie is most often described as a large animal with a long, slender neck attached to a small, serpent-like head. It has a body shaped like that of a seal, only bigger and thicker. Some reports and sightings have claimed that it has a slight hump on its back, which protrudes from the waters as it swims on the surface. It has four limbs that resemble flippers, like a seal's, and it has a tail as long as its neck but thinner.

Nessie, as depicted in Popular Culture

Throughout the world, the popularity of Nessie has grown tremendously, despite its somewhat mythical nature. The creature is depicted and referenced heavily in popular culture. Nessie appears as a mysterious, benevolent monster in literature pieces, such as books, short story publications, poems, comics, in newspapers, and even in tabloids. Authors, like the famous *J.K. Rowling*, creator of the *Harry Potter* series, has featured the monster prominently in her 2001 book, *Fantastic Beasts and Where to Find Them.*

Movies and television also pay their share of homages to Nessie. Countless monster movies, documentaries, historical specials, and cameos have depicted the Loch Ness Monster as a larger-than-life creature. In the highly popular Disney-Pixar film *Monsters Inc.*, Nessie is part of the mythology of their world, being a monster that was banished from the monsters' city. In television, Nessie has made appearances on popular cartoons like *Jimmy Neutron, Phineas and Ferb, Futurama,* and *Sailor Moon.*

People's fascination with Nessie extends to far more than shallow curiosity. Although there has not yet been ample evidence to support its existence, history and lore seem to play a huge part in the mystique and legend of this creature. Perhaps it is worth taking a look at the origin of the myth to get to know the real beginnings of the "Loch Ness Monster."

Chapter 2:

Origins and Sightings

The Story of St. Columba

The supposedly earliest known sighting of Nessie dates back to the year 565 A.D., although the events were documented a full century after their occurrence. In *Adamnan of Iona*'s book, *Life of St. Columba*, the iconic monk describes a monster that lives in Loch Ness.

According to the story, an Irish monk named St. Columba was visiting the land of the Picts when he and his companions came upon the locals who were busy burying their kin by the shores of the River Ness. When they inquired about the fate of the deceased man, they were told that he had been savagely attacked by a "water beast" and had been dragged under the water to drown. When the locals saw the attack, they immediately got into their boats and headed for the man, attempting to save him but they were too late. The man was already dead by the time they got to him, so they dragged his corpse to shore in order to give him a proper burial.

After he heard their story, St. Columba bid his follower, Luigne moccu Min, to swim in the river. The crowd was very surprised at his command, but when his follower did swim across, the beast came after him. St. Columba then made the sign of the Cross and addressed the beast, "Go no further. Do not touch the man. Go back at once." Immediately, the beast halted as if it had gotten tangled and pulled back with ropes. The monster fled in terror, and Columba, his men, and the Picts praised God for the miracle.

The Dr. Mackenzie Sighting of 1871

Dr. Mackenzie of Balnain was a young lad at the time when he happened to be passing by the Loch. A movement on the surface of the lake caught his eye. He said he noticed an object that very much looked like a log or an upturned boat that appeared to be, in his own words, "wriggling and churning up the water." He tried to move in for a closer look but the object started to move, slowly at first, then it took off for the deeper waters at a much faster speed.

Dr. Mackenzie never mentioned his experience to anyone for years, until other people began to report their sightings in 1934. He wrote a letter to his friend Rupert Gould, a lieutenant commander in the British Royal Navy, detailing his   story.

The Spicer Couple, Arthur Grant

In July of 1933, George Spicer and his wife were driving on a road near the loch when they came across a massive creature blocking their way. They immediately stopped the car right in front of it. The creature had a large body about four feet high and twenty-five feet long, and it had a long, narrow neck that they both compared to an elephant's trunk but slightly thicker. The neck, they figured, was as long as the width of the road, later measured to be about twelve feet wide. They described the neck as having curious undulations on it.

The Spicers did not get to see the creature's limbs because they were inside the car and a dip in the road obscured them. It staggered as it crossed the road and headed for the loch, which was about twenty yards away. It left a trail of crushed undergrowth as it lurched and they saw it enter the water and disappear shortly after.

A month later, a young motorcyclist and veterinary student, named Arthur Grant, was also speeding along a road near the Loch at night. When he was approaching Abriachan following the northeastern shore, he almost crashed when he saw the monster trying to cross the road in front of him. It also saw him with its small head and quickly retreated back to the loch. Grant got off his bike and ran after the creature. He followed it to the loch but barely missed its dive, only seeing the ripples in its wake. When pressed for a description, Grant said that it looked like it was a hybrid between a seal and a plesiosaur.

Both of these incidents happened on a new road that was built along the loch in early 1933. Its opening had brought all sorts of people into the formerly secluded area. Announced sightings of the monster have steadily increased since then.

The Hugh Gray Photograph

In November of 1933, just three months after the Arthur Grant sighting, a man by the name of Hugh Gray came to be walking along the shores of the Loch right after he had gone to church. He was suddenly surprised by a commotion in the water only a couple of yards away from him. A creature revealed itself to be the source of the commotion when it rose up out of the water. Gray, for whatever reason, had brought his camera at the time, so he started taking several pictures. Later, it was found that only one of them had developed and the picture was very blurry, suggesting that the creature was thrashing about.

In the picture, there seemed to be a thick-bodied creature with stumpy limbs on its sides. Upon closer inspection, an eel-like face and head could be seen on the far right side of the image.

Critics of the photograph suggest an alternate explanation - the creature on the picture was Gray's Labrador retriever carrying a stick and making splashes while swimming. People are still debating on which of this explanation is the correct one, as compelling cases can be made for both   sides.

The Iconic "Surgeon's Photograph"

The "Surgeon's Photograph" was named so because the man who took the photograph, a London gynecologist named Robert Kenneth Wilson, did not want to be associated with it. In 1934, Wilson was staring at the loch when he saw a creature pop out of the water. He grabbed his camera and took four photos, but, just like the Gray photos, he later discovered that only two of them developed well enough to be discernible.

The first photo shows the creature popping out of the lake, its long narrow neck standing mostly upright with its back exposed. The second photo shows the head going into a diving position. The inherent quality and easy interpretability of the first photo made it iconic. However, the second one was a little blurry and hard to interpret, so it attracted lesser publicity.

Skeptics have tried to explain the photo pointing to other possible suspects as to what the creature might be. Some believed that it was merely a piece of driftwood, or an otter or a bird, and some even believe it to be the snout of a submerged elephant. There were further analyses of the photograph that showed that the object was quite small and only measured about two to three feet long. However, other analyses concentrating on the size proved to be inconsistent and unreliable.

The Taylor film of 1938

A South African tourist by the name of G.E. Taylor was filming the loch when he noticed something in the water. He began filming the disturbance, following its slow, straight wake with his camera. Taylor managed to capture over three minutes of the incident on a 16mm color film. He then gave the film to British zoologist, Maurice Burton, for safekeeping.

When Burton was pressed to show the film, he refused. A single frame was later published on his book, *The Elusive Monster*.

C.B. Farrel Sighting

One C.B. Farrel of the Royal Observer Corps (ROC) claimed to have been distracted from his duties by something coming out of the loch in May of 1943. He was approximately 750 feet away from the water when a creature with a long four-foot neck and a body thirty feet long popped out of the loch. It had large eyes and prominent fins on its body.

Something Gets Picked up on Sonar

In December of 1954, a fishing boat named *Rival III* was sailing out on the loch, as the crew was looking for schools of fish with their sonar. The crew observed a large object that was detected by the sonar on their viewfinder. It was keeping pace with the boat and following them at a depth of about 480 feet. It followed them for nearly 2,600 feet before it disappeared from radar. They tried to recapture the signal and after a few minutes it came back. Then it disappeared again—this time, for good.

Since then, a lot of people have been scouring the loch with sonar, attempting to recreate what the crew had detected that day.

The Dinsdale Footage

Tim Dinsdale was an aeronautical engineer who served in the Royal Air Force. He was also a famous believer in the existence of Nessie. In April of 1960, he set out to Loch Ness to prove the creature's existence and had with him nearly fifty feet of film, expecting to fully capture and document it once and for all.

For four days, he scoured the edges of the Loch, watching, waiting, and trying to find any shred of evidence of unidentified animals that might have dwelt there. He never found any.

While he was having breakfast near the loch on the fifth day, he supposedly saw a huge creature swimming and making waves in the loch. It was diving and coming back up again, its body rolled around the surface of the water, creating waves. By the time Dinsdale had grabbed his camera and had gone closer to film it, the creature was already retreating. He only got to film a hump gliding across the water, making a powerful wake that was different from any man-made boat. Dinsdale filmed the creature for nearly a minute.

To this day, that film is considered by many Nessie believers/advocates to be near-definitive proof that Nessie exists. The Joint Air Reconnaissance Intelligence Centre, also known as JARIC, an organization under the United Kingdom Defense Intelligence, analyzed the film and believed that the object was "probably animate."

A computer expert commissioned by Discovery Communications as a resource for their documentary, *Loch Ness Discovered*, enhanced the film and examined its validity. He noted a prominent underwater shadow that was not naturally obvious in the original footage. Later, he commented, "Before I saw the film, I thought the Loch Ness Monster was a load of rubbish. Having done the enhancement, I'm not so sure [anymore]."

Skeptics counter this evidence by claiming that an overturned boat could have easily produced the same effect of the object. Also, the shadow, they say, was merely undisturbed water that was coincidentally formed into the shape of a body.

A More Recent Footage

In May of 2007, Gordon Holmes went to the loch and took some footage of something moving across the water. The 55 year old lab technician described the creature as being jet black and very long, about 50 feet from front to end. It had a fairly fast speed as it glided just underneath the surface of the loch.

A marine biologist named Adrian Shine, who was working at the Loch Ness 2000 Centre in Drumnadrochit, was shown the footage and declared it to be among the best footage of Nessie he'd ever seen. Later though, in another interview with STV News' North Tonight, the same Adrian Shine implicitly retracted his previous statement by suggesting that the footage was that of a seal, otter or some kind of water   bird.

Sonar gets another Ping

A local Loch Ness ship captain detected something curious on his sonar in August of 2011. Marcus Atkinson took a picture of his sonar screen, revealing an image of a five-foot wide unidentified object that was following his boat for two straight minutes. It looked to be swimming at a depth of seventy-five feet, and he concluded that the creature was definitely not a fish or a seal.

A year later, scientists from the National Oceanography Centre examined the photograph and they concluded that it was some sort of algae bloom or zooplankton. Roland Watson, a cryptozoologist, disagreed with their findings, stating that algae would not have the ability to grow because they needed sunlight and the waters of Loch Ness are very dark, especially at a depth of seventy-five feet.

A Mysterious Wave Appears

A five-minute video, taken by a tourist named David Elder in August of 2013, features a mysterious dark wave traveling on the surface of the Loch. The 50-year old Elder was just taking a picture of a swan near the shore when he noticed the movement in the background. He speculated that underneath the wave was a fifteen-foot "solid black object" responsible for its creation. He further described the wave as being quiet, with no ripples coming off of it and the water surrounding it being very still.

Skeptics believe the mysterious wave to be the product of a simple gust of wind.

The Latest from Apple Maps

In April of 2014, a man by the name of Andrew Dixon was browsing Apple Maps from his home and decided to take a look at Loch Ness. To his surprise, he saw what appeared to be the silhouette of a giant creature swimming close to the surface.

Some people have pointed out that a boat creating a wake could attain the same effect. Photoshop could also be a possible culprit, as the image looks suspiciously like the silhouette of a whale   shark.

Chapter 3:

Possible Explanations

As with all legends, the story of Nessie could possibly have its roots in reality, obscured and misshapen by time, different eyewitness accounts, or natural phenomena. Here are a few theories as to what Nessie really is.

Trees: More *Bark* than Bite

Recently, comparing and contrasting the presence of trees around a loch, and the lochs that have garnered monster legends over the years, has led to an interesting correlation. It seems that only those lochs with pinewoods on their shores have been associated with monster legends, such as Kelpies and Nessie. This might point to a possible explanation for most Nessie sightings.

Way back in 1933, the Daily Mirror published a photograph of an unconventional-looking tree trunk that had been floating in the loch and washed ashore in the Scottish village of Foyers. The caption basically speculated that the said tree trunk was the source of all the reported sightings of a "monster" in the lake at that time.

Dr. Maurice Burton has pegged Scots Pine, a type of pine native to northern Europe and Asia and common on the shores of a number of lochs in Scotland, including Loch Ness, as the main culprit of most misidentifications and Nessie sightings, in a series of articles for *New Scientist* in 1982.

Burton proposed that the high levels of resin found on the pine would actually prevent the gases resultant of its decaying process from exiting the body of the tree initially. Eventually, though, the rising pressure of the gases would cause a rupture at the end of the fermenting log and propel it forward, making it look like a creature swimming through the water. The shape of the common branch stumps, he added, closely resembled some of the descriptions of Nessie's limbs.

The fermentation and decaying processes of the floating logs would also explain the frothy wake most sightings describe. Surfactants and other gaseous by-products caused by the decay would bring about this phenomenon.

Still, some believers assert that there are lochs that have legends of monsters, despite the absence of pinewoods or any kind of tree growing on their shores.

Seismic Gas Theory Isn't Just A Bunch of Hot Air

Rare coincidences involving geological phenomena may explain many of the Nessie sightings and stories, proposes Italian geologist Luigi Piccardi. The Loch Ness is incidentally located along the Great Glen Fault. So, Piccardi suggests that the earliest sighting of Nessie might have been an earthquake caused by the fault's movements.

As mentioned earlier, the first recorded sighting of Nessie was in the book, *Life of St. Columba*. It was described that the creature emerged from the waters with a very loud roaring. This great "roaring" might be interpreted as describing the sounds of an earthquake. Furthermore, a release of previously trapped gases underneath the loch by said earthquake might produce a bubble of gas that exits as a disturbance on the water. This would definitely create wakes and ripples, along with foamy bubbles, and could be mistaken for a large creature swimming below the surface.

Normal but Intriguing: Wakes and Seiches

A seiche occurs when water is blown into one end of the lake and races back like a standing wave attempting to revert to its natural level. This regular lake oscillation is a common occurrence in most lochs but can be very perplexing to those who aren't familiar with it, as the waves seem to appear without apparent causes. Tourists and common folk might associate these mysterious waves as the product of some unseen creature swimming underneath the surface of the water.

Boat wakes may also give the impression that they are produced by something unseen because most wakes travel at a considerable distance throughout the body of water and have the tendency to deflect on the sides of the boat, causing larger wakes than the one originally produced. Once the wakes reach the shore, the boat may have already passed from view, leaving people to wonder what made these unusual wakes in the first place.

Natural Illusions and Optical Effects

Occasionally, gusts of wind blowing on the calm surface of a loch can produce a very unusual matte appearance, which are accompanied by calm patches that seem like dark oval shadows if viewed far enough, or from the shore.

Reflections from the nearby hills and faraway mountains can also appear as humps to the unfamiliar tourists. Atmospheric refraction, the same phenomenon responsible for mirages, could distort the shapes of common objects or animals that are indigenous to the loch, thus making them appear strange and menacing.

If It Looks Like A Seal, It Probably Is

In 1934, an amateur expedition led by Sir Edward Mountain analyzed various film footages that were taken the same year and came to the conclusion that the monster was in fact a species of seal. There are a number of photographic and film evidence that confirm the presence of seals in the loch during several months of the year. Their findings were published in a national newspaper with the headline, "Loch Ness Riddle Solved – Official."

Both R.T. Gould and renowned Irish author, Peter Costello, came to the conclusion that a long-necked seal, most likely a grey seal, was the animal mistaken for Nessie. Grey seals have surprisingly long and extensible necks, they swim in a fashion and have flippers that are similar to what most Nessie sightings describe, and they do occasionally waddle from the shores and onto the roads. Furthermore, these creatures could account for the animated sonar detections.

There are arguments against this theory that put forth the fact that all species of seals usually sunbathe during daylight hours and are fully visible on land, thus making it hard for people to mistake these creatures as Nessie. Also, the seals from Loch Ness are observed to be quite infrequent, suggesting that their populations are only visiting rather that establishing a permanent   colony.

Birds Also Get The Blame

A local bartender, David Munro, claims that he witnessed an unmistakable disturbance in the water—a wide wake that seemed to be diving and resurfacing, zigzagging as it glided across the surface. Twenty-six other witnesses confirmed his sighting, describing a V-shaped wake, too wide to have been made by a boat. This phenomenon happened while the loch was dead calm, with no boat present and no strong gusts of wind.

Under the same calm conditions, creatures too small to be seen from the shore can leave big V-shaped wakes, especially if they travel in groups. A flock of birds, in particular, do sometimes travel in V-shaped formations. Once they collectively land on the calm water or disturb the surface in any way, a similar wake may be produced. They can also all leave the water together, producing an even more prominent wake and then land again. This gives the illusion of something wading in the water or breaking out of it.

Giant Eels?

There are a number of eel species in Loch Ness, which may explain some of the Nessie sightings that have been reported. The Conger eel species, specifically, are abundant in lochs throughout Scotland, including Loch Ness. These congers have an average length of sixty inches, but the biggest of them could reach 10 feet. They can also weigh up to 240 lbs., which would make them the largest eels in the world—a prime candidate as far as Nessie sightings are concerned.

In 1856, reported sightings of sea serpents, or Kelpies, in a loch near the village of Leurbost in the Outer Hebrides were explained as a misidentification of an oversized eel, which were also common in those lakes.

Most people who are skeptical of this explanation often point out that eels do not have the capacity to protrude their heads above water in a swan-like manner, like most of the Nessie sightings have described, and therefore cannot possibly account for those occasions. The same sightings also describe a swimming pattern of diving and rising back up to the surface, like a seal, making the eels a lesser candidate because they swim in a side-to-side undulation.

The Occasional Circus Elephant

In 2006, the artist and paleontologist, Neil Clark, proposed that travelling circuses around the area might have sent their elephants for a swim on the loch, and that their submerged bodies and their protruding trunks might have had people mistaking them for Nessie. The elephant's trunk, which it uses as a snorkel, could very well fit most descriptions of Nessie sightings for a swanlike head and neck, and its partially surfacing back of the head could be taken for a hump.

This is particularly compelling evidence to some people, considering that in 1979, geographer Donald Johnson and biologist Dennis Power claimed that the famous Surgeon's Photograph was in fact a submerged elephant with its trunk sticking out. Most people would attest that, upon examining the picture in detail, with this particular explanation in mind, the resemblance is   quite   uncanny.

Greenland Shark: A Monster Hunter's Take On The Legend

Jeremy Wade, a popular angler and host of the television show, *River Monsters*, investigated the legend of the Loch Ness Monster in 2013 as a part of his series. The fifty-nine year old biologist came to the conclusion that the creature of legend was most likely a very large Greenland shark.

Greenland sharks are large sharks that are native to the waters of the North Atlantic. These sharks prefer to live farther north than any other species of shark, and they can grow up to twenty feet in length. They are mostly dark in color, and they lack the distinctive dorsal fin of most sharks. These sharks are also known to have the most toxic meat of any shark in the world, as they have a high content of urea in their meat.

It is speculated that these sharks could live and thrive in fresh water by using lakes and rivers to acquire food. Loch Ness has an abundance of fish, including salmon.

Tall Tales And Myths From Folklore

Bengt Sjögren, a Swedish naturalist, postulates that the legend of the Loch Ness Monster, and indeed all other lake monsters, evolved from the earlier legends of the Kelpies. He supports this theory by bringing to light the fact that descriptions of Nessie have steadily changed over the years, originally describing the creature to be horse-like in appearance.

A Kelpie is a mythical shape-shifting water spirit that often takes the form of a horse. Legends say that it would come out of the water to look for tired travelers. When the traveler gets on the back of the Kelpie, it would gallop back into the loch, dive in, and devour its unfortunate prey.

This old myth was intended to keep children away from the loch. Sjögren believes that this old legend has merged with the modern awareness of plesiosaurs to create the contemporary legend of Nessie.

Believers argue that the witnesses from long ago would only have been able to describe Nessie through comparing it with creatures that they were already familiar with. Seeing as plesiosaurs were not yet discovered until the early 1600s, they might have compared Nessie to horses.

The *Real* Hoaxes

There have been many attempts at hoaxes since the Loch Ness Monster became popular in the 1930s. The possibility that most, if not all, of these sightings are a product of an elaborate hoax, or a combination of discreet hoaxes, realistically cannot be ignored.

There were a couple of major hoaxes in the past that have since been exposed. So, here are a few.

A big-game hunter by the name of Marmaduke Wetherell visited Loch Ness to try to find Nessie in 1930. He claimed to have found huge footprints of the creature. However, when casts of the prints were sent to scientists for analysis, they were revealed to be the footprints of a hippopotamus. Wetherell had likely placed the prints himself using a hippopotamus-foot umbrella stand.

In 1959, an Italian journalist, Francesco Gasparini, reported that a large, strange fish had been found on the lake. He later fabricated reports of eyewitnesses corroborating his story and upgrading the description of the fish into that of a monster, as he thought a fish would not yield a long article.

One Gerald McSorely supposedly found a fossil that belonged to Nessie in 2003. After a thorough investigation, it was determined that he had placed the fossil beforehand and that it was not originally from Loch Ness.

An animatronic model of a realistic-looking plesiosaur was constructed in 2004 by a documentary crew in the hopes of making people believe that there was something in Loch Ness. The animatronic model, affectionately named "Lucy," did her job and about six hundred sightings were reported on that single day.

In 2005, two local students claimed to have found a tooth embedded into a deer carcass that had been washed ashore. They set up a website and publicized the "tooth" widely, but subsequent expert analysis revealed that the tooth was actually the tip of a muntjac antler. It was later found out that the whole thing had been a publicity stunt to promote a horror novel.

A video posted on YouTube in 2007 showed Nessie breaching into the air. Later, it was revealed that the video had been a viral ad promotingan upcoming movie, *The Water Horse* by Sony Pictures.

The Famous Plesiosaur Theory

It was suggested since the early 1930s that Nessie could possibly a Plesiosaur—a supposedly extinct long-necked aquatic reptile that lived during the Triassic and Cretaceous periods.

There are a number of arguments that have been put against this theory. So, here are a few.

Plesiosaurs were most likely cold-blooded reptiles that required warmer tropical waters to survive. The average temperature of Loch Ness only gets to about 5.5 degrees Celsius, which means that even if these Plesiosaurs were warm-blooded thzt they would require a food supply much larger than the loch can provide to survive.

Plesiosaurs were also found out not to be able to lift their necks into a swan-like position, as most Nessie sightings describe.

The Loch Ness is a relatively young body of water, geologically speaking. At only 10,000 years old, the loch was nothing more than a solid piece of frozen ice 20,000 years before it thawed.

If creatures that were similar to Plesiosaurs did happen to live on Loch Ness, they would have to have been seen fairly frequently because of their constant need to surface to breathe.

These criticisms also have a fair rebuttal proposed by Tim Dinsdale, Roy Mackal, and Peter Scott. They theorize that a distinct marine creature evolved either from the Plesiosaur, or from another completely separate organism that evolved into a shape similar to that of a Plesiosaur by convergent evolution, was trapped in the lake long ago and has since thrived there.

Conclusion

I hope this short, concise book was able to give you a definitive glimpse into the mysterious legend of the Loch Ness Monster. The legend of Nessie has always been a very interesting subject, and by looking at its aspects in great detail, most of us can agree that there is a certain truth that we have come to learn from it - despite the advancements of man, the world is still a magical and mysterious place, full of possibilities.

The next step is to hopefully foster the feeling of wonder that you have gained from reading this book and continue to read other articles about Nessie and all other cryptids. Through the Internet and other modern means of learning, the world has become more accessible but *not* less mysterious.

Finally, if you learned something from this book, please take the time to share your thoughts by sending me a message or even posting a review to Amazon.

CPSIA information can be obtained
at www.ICGtesting.com
Printed in the USA
LVOW13s2041221116
514101LV00021B/265/P